THE DRAGON'S LAIR

AN EROTIC FAIRYTALE

VICTORIA RUSH

VOLUME 3

CLOVER'S FANTASY ADVENTURES -
BOOK 3

COPYRIGHT

For the uninhibited...

WANT TO AMP UP YOUR SEX LIFE?

Sign up for my newsletter to receive more free books and other steamy stuff. Discover a hundred different ways to wet your whistle!

Victoria Rush Erotica

1
———

"So where do you want to go next?" Jessop said as he climbed onto Rex's back with his two friends.

"The days are starting to get shorter," Clover said, pulling back on the dragon's ears, directing him to take flight. "What do you say we head south toward warmer climes?"

As the animal soared skyward, the trio peered over his flapping wings at the tall trees in the land of giants.

"Where do you think we'll be able to find a mate for Rex?" Tara said, clasping her arms around Clover's waist for support. "The last time we stumbled upon one was deep in the forest. How do you expect to find another one way up here?"

"Dragon's *fly*, right?" Clover said, peering over her shoulder at her elf friend. "It stands to reason we have a better chance of finding one up in the air than on the ground. They're pretty hard to miss once they take flight."

Tara swiveled her head, scanning the horizon in every direction.

"There's nothing but open sky for hundreds of miles

around. How do we even know there's another dragon anywhere near here? They're kind of rare, after all."

Clover saw a tall mountain range a few miles to the east and tilted her body to point Rex in that direction.

"Don't they usually hang out on high ground? Every fairy tale I ever read always had the dragon's lair on some craggy mountaintop."

"You and your fairy tales," Tara said, shaking her head.

As Rex angled higher above the treetops, the trio looked down at the changing landscape. The higher the land rose up from the sea, the thicker the brush became. As the trees changed from widely spaced redwoods to more closely packed pines and cedars, the rising hillsides became awash in green, woven with slivers of silver as tumbling waterfalls carved their way through the dense canopy toward the bright ocean shimmering in the afternoon sunlight.

It was a magical sight from so far above the ground, and Clover smiled as she felt the warm breeze ruffling through her hair. It had only been a little over a week since she'd tumbled into this fantasy land of Abbynthia, and after so many exciting adventures in the short time she'd been here, she could scarcely remember her boring life back in Tennessee.

"Do you feel like a refreshing shower?" Tara said, pointing toward a large waterfall a few hundred feet to their left as her fingers caressed Clover's exposed belly. "It's been a while since we had a bath, and I'm still sticky from the king's cum all over my body. Besides, you never know, maybe this is where you'll find another portal to take you home."

"I'm not sure I *want* to anymore," Clover said, watching the sun tracing lower on the horizon. "I'm having way too much fun hanging out you guys. But I definitely think we could do with a little clean-up before we turn in for the day."

Clover leaned her body forward and pulled on Rex's left ear, steering him in the direction of the waterfall, and he landed softly on an embankment a few feet below the cascade. As he knelt down to let the trio disembark, she felt the spray from the cataract showering over her body and she closed her eyes while she opened her mouth, tasting the fresh elixir.

"Mmm," she sighed. "It's been a while since I've been under one of these things."

"And it's been a while since you've had sex with someone your own *size*," Tara grinned, removing her frock and placing her bow on the river bank. She glanced over at Jessop, who'd already removed his clothes and was sporting a half-woody peering at the sexy elf's naked body. "It looks like I'm not the *only* one eager to feel the skin of a normal human for a change."

"Is that right, Jessop?" Clover said, peering at his erection flapping up against his belly. "Are you ready to feel the touch of a woman's pussy after rubbing up against the king's giant pecker?"

"I think I've had plenty enough *dick* for a while," Jessop said, wiping the king's cum off his body from the overhead spray.

"Speak for yourself," Clover smiled, grabbing his pole and leading him under the falling water.

When they entered the cascade, the three friends quickly melded together, kissing each other passionately while their hands roamed over their bodies. As they began rubbing their private parts together, they moaned into each other's mouths while the waterfall washed their bodies clean of the vestiges of the king and queen's sexual emissions. It didn't take long for the trio to begin shaking and climaxing in each other's arms, and after they finished coming, they stumbled out from under the cataract, lying exhausted on the river bank in the afternoon sun.

"Are you disappointed the waterfall didn't take you back to Asheville?" Tara said, reflecting back on how Clover had fallen into her new world.

"Not really," Clover said, smiling at Rex snoring contentedly beside them on the embankment. "I'm not ready to return home anyway. I left because I wasn't happy with my lonely life and my parent's expectations of me. Here, I can do whatever I want and go anywhere I please. Plus, the airfare's a lot cheaper..."

"Airfare?" Tara said, looking at Clover with a puzzled expression.

"Where I come from," she smiled. "People fly through the air in giant machines that use jet engines to provide propulsion. Rex is a lot more environmentally friendly and more fun to ride. I'm kind of getting used to roughing it in your world."

"We seem to be managing just fine with our old-fashioned tools," Tara said, lifting her bow in the air.

"I wouldn't have it any other way," Clover laughed, reaching over to clasp Tara's hand. "To paraphrase a famous poet from my world, all I need is a bit of sustenance and the company of some good friends."

"Hey!" Jessop said, suddenly sitting up and cocking his head. "Do you guys hear that strange sound?"

Tara and Clover sat up beside him and tilted their heads, furrowing their brows in concentration. They heard a faint screeching sound coming from further up the mountainside. Suddenly Rex jerked awake and began flapping his wings excitedly, growling like he sensed danger.

"What is it, boy?" Clover said, peering over at him. "What's that sound?"

"It better not be any more of those *gargoyles*," Jessop said, shaking his head. "We're kind of exposed down here on the ground."

"I agree," Clover said. "We can get a better idea of what's going on up in the air. Let's get dressed and check it out."

The three friends put their clothes back on then climbed atop Rex's back, and he quickly took flight, heading in the direction of the screeching sound. As they scaled the mountain in the direction of a rocky outcropping, they noticed some unusual movement outside a large cave.

"Look!" Tara said, pointing toward the hollow. "It's another dragon!"

"Yes," Clover said, squinting her eyes. "And it seems to be agitated by something."

"Let's hope it's not by the sight of another dragon rapidly approaching with three strange humans riding on its back," Jessop said.

"I don't think it's *us* he's worried about," Clover said, pointing toward a band of men waving bows and spears below the dragon.

"They're firing arrows at it!" Tara said. "And it seems injured. I don't think it can escape!"

As Rex swooped in on the band, they pointed their bows at the interloper, firing a fusillade of arrows over the trio's heads. The dragon angled toward them, unleashing a stream of fire in their direction, but they retreated behind a cluster of boulders, shielding them from the attack.

"There's too many of them," Jessop said. "Rex's fire can't reach them in their hiding places."

"We're going to have to flush them out," Clover said, steering Rex onto the cliff beside the injured dragon. "You stay here and protect your friend," she said as Tara and Jessop crept into the surrounding bush on opposite sides of the outcropping. "We'll see if we can drive them out of their holes."

Then Clover crawled down to join her friend near where the band was holed up.

"Are you sure this is a good idea?" Tara said, shaking her head at Clover. "There seems to be a lot more of them than us."

"We just need to scare them out of their hiding places," Clover said. "Rex will take care of the rest."

As they crept closer to the cluster of boulders, they saw a group of five men crouching in the shadows. Tara pulled her bow off her back and began firing arrows in their direction. As they curled back around the large stones, Jessop suddenly appeared from the other side, attacking them with his sword. When they realized they were trapped on both sides, they stepped back from the hollow, whereupon Rex let loose with a giant hail of fire. The men screamed in terror, retreating into the woods as the flailed at their burning clothes. After waiting a few minutes to make sure the men weren't going to return, the three friends joined back together, looking at each other anxiously.

"Do you think they're gone for good?" Jessop said.

"I can't imagine they'll be coming back anytime soon with two fire-breathing dragons bringing infantry support," Clover said. "Let's go see what's going on with the other dragon."

As they climbed back up onto the ledge, the wounded dragon hissed at them, rearing up as he prepared to fire at them. But Rex stepped in front of him and spread his wings as if to signal that they weren't a threat. The other dragon eased back down on its haunches while he peered at the approaching group, growling softly.

Tara placed her bow on the ground and tiptoed slowly toward the animal, holding out her hands to show that she meant no harm. When she got next to Rex, she patted the side of his face and he purred to signal his friendship with the humans. The other dragon peered at Rex then back towards Tara, tilting its head, unsure what to make of her. As she crept closer toward the wounded animal, her eyes widened when she saw two large arrows embedded in the side of its belly.

"Is he alright?" Clover said. "Can you see if he's hurt?"

"It's been hit by a couple of arrows, but they don't look life-threatening. And it appears to be a *she*, not a he."

"Can you patch her up like you did with Rex a few days ago?"

"I think so," Tara said, inching closer to the animal while patting the side of its mouth gently. "But we're going to have to administer another dose of anesthetic to put her to sleep. I don't think she's going to take too kindly to my trying to pull those arrows out of her flesh."

Clover nodded, noticing the dragon beginning to relax.

"You stay there and keep making friends while Jessop and I look for the necessary ingredients."

"Keep an eye out for any other dragonslayers hiding in the woods," Tara said. "The last thing I need is to be stranded up here alone with two angry hydras."

"Not to worry," Clover said, noticing Rex scanning the brush for any other sign of danger. "We'll be back soon. It looks like Rex has got your back in the meantime."

2

When Clover and Jessop returned with their provisions from the surrounding brush, Tara knelt down and built a small fire with some kindling and broken logs. Then she placed a few large rocks around the fire and positioned a hollowed-out bowl above the pit, pouring some fresh water into the pot. When the water came to a boil, she sprinkled in the last of the sleep potion she'd taken from the warlock's cabin, fanning the smoke away from her.

"Are you sure this is going to work?" Clover said, peering at the injured dragon anxiously.

"Assuming there's enough sleep potion to put her out," Tara nodded. "But we can't afford to waste any of the serum. You know the drill."

"You mean...?" Clover said, remembering what she'd had to do the last time they put Rex to sleep when they found him similarly disabled.

"You've got the largest bodysuit. Fan the vapor in the dragon's direction."

Clover dutifully removed her sheepskin outfit and began flapping the cloth over the fire, sending the smoke and fumes toward the two dragons. After a few minutes, they collapsed onto the ground with their mouths wide agape.

"That stuff sure is powerful," Jessop said, circling around the fire to stay upwind of the fumes.

"At least that warlock was good for *something*," Tara nodded. "Why don't you guys keep a lookout for more intruders while I get to work removing these arrows?"

While Clover and Jessop scanned the woods for any further sign of activity, Tara knelt down in front of the injured dragon, using her hunting knife to slice away the flesh around the entrance wounds, then she slowly pulled the spears out of its body. After applying a soothing aloe balm, she stitched up the wounds and joined her friends on the edge of the overlook watching the sun setting over the sea.

"All good?" Clover said.

"I think so," Tara nodded. "The dragon's scales stopped the spears from going in too far. As long as there isn't any internal damage, she should heal up in a few days good as new."

"Are *all* elves this resourceful?" Clover smiled, caressing the inside of Tara's thigh.

"We learn from an early age to take care of ourselves," she said. "Not everyone is lucky enough to be born in a place with electricity and flying machines."

"You should see some of the *other* machines modern technology has invented," Clover said, tracing her fingers further up between Tara's legs.

"Maybe someday you can take us back there to experience all this wonderful technology," Tara said, pushing Clover's hand away from her crotch. "But for the time being,

I think we should keep our wits about us in case those savages get any more ideas. Why don't you two try to catch some sleep while I take the first watch?"

"I can definitely do with a few zzz's after that ordeal at the king's castle," Clover nodded. "What's our plan for tomorrow?"

"The other dragon must be hungry after fighting off those attackers, and she won't be able to fly for a few days. We'll have to scrounge up some food, then look for a new hiding place. Something tells me there'll be more of those dragonslayers where they came from. It won't take long for the word to get out that there's two of them holed up in this mountain dugout."

For the next few days, the three friends tended to the injured dragon's wounds, catching wild game and boar to keep them fed while keeping a lookout for any more dragonslayers. The new dragon seemed to be getting more comfortable in Rex's presence and watched with bemusement whenever Clover climbed atop his back to scan the surrounding landscape. After a week or so, the trio awoke to the sound of loud grunting and noticed Rex humping his new friend while she panted excitedly.

"Looks like Rex finally found that piece of ass he was looking for," Jessop kidded, nudging Clover in the side.

"Thank heavens," she said. "I was afraid he was going to poke one of *us* with his giant tool if he didn't find a suitable mate soon."

"It looks like his girlfriend is healing up nicely," Tara nodded, watching her heaving flanks as Rex emptied his seed inside her. "She should be ready to fly again pretty soon."

"Are you thinking about taking her for a test drive?" Clover said.

"It's better to have *two* trained dragons than one with all these troublemakers floating around. Besides, I've been a bit envious watching you taking the lead with Rex all this time."

"How come *Tara* gets to have the front seat again?" Jessop said, frowning. "Where I come from, the *men* are always in charge of the animals!"

"You come from a place where lords and bishops are in charge," Tara said, noticing the new dragon purring contentedly against her thigh. "Out here in the wild, men and women equal. Besides, this new dragon seems to have taken a liking to me."

"Humpf!" Jessop grunted, crossing his arms over his chest.

"Who knows?" Clover kidded. "At this rate, maybe you'll find a dragon of your *own* before too long. Then *nobody* would want to mess with us!"

"If we're going to take this one with us," Tara said, stroking the dragon's head gently, "I suppose we should give her a name. Have you got any more bright ideas from your so-called fairy tales?"

Clover paused for a moment to think about her favorite stories, then she smiled.

"There's a funny tale about a giant ogre and his sidekick donkey who adopt an amorous dragon as their friend. They named her Elizabeth, or Betty for short."

"*Rex and Betty*," Tara nodded, watching the new dragon rubbing her haunches against Rex's back leg. "It's got a nice ring to it. And she seems to fit the part. She might be even hornier than *you*, Clover, if that's even possible."

"Why don't you see if you can channel that energy while she's still in a friendly mood?" Clover smiled. "Maybe she's ready for a different kind of ride."

Tara raised herself up and patted the back of the dragon's neck, slowly moving down her back.

"What do you say, Betty?" she said. "Do you want to see what it's like to have a *human* riding your back for a change?"

The dragon growled as Tara pressed her foot onto its side and climbed up onto its back. At first, she tried to throw Tara off by shaking its hips from side to side, but the elf held tightly onto the bony spurs on the back of its neck and after a few seconds it rose up slowly, flapping its wings softly.

"That's it, girl," Tara said, patting the side of its neck gently. "I'm your friend, remember? You keep me out of harm's way and I'll do the same. Are you ready to try out your wings?"

The dragon began flapping its wings more forcefully, then it leaped off the side of the ledge, gliding rapidly over the treetops in the direction of the sea. After a short while, it began angling and diving playfully with Tara holding on for dear life.

"We better go make sure she doesn't kill herself," Clover said, jumping on Rex's back. "Come on, let's join in the fun!"

Jessop hopped on behind Clover, then Rex took off after the other pair, swooping down beside them.

"*Woo-hoo!*" Tara shouted happily as the dragons arced and soared together in tandem, following the rolling terrain of the ruffled mountainside.

It didn't take Tara long to figure out how to steer her dragon using the signals she'd learned watching Clover with Rex, and after ten minutes of playful dancing over the undulating hillsides, the two dragons resumed a steady course flying alongside one another at the side of the seashore.

"Do you have any idea where you're going?" Clover yelled, pulling up alongside Tara.

"I'm not sure," Tara said. "Somewhere far away from here."

She peered out over the sea, noticing a small dot far on the horizon.

"How about that island far offshore? It might provide a bit more shelter from the dragonslayers."

"Works for me," Clover nodded. "Lead the way."

Tara tilted her body toward the open sea, tugging gently on her dragon's right ear, angling southwest in the direction of the island.

"Looks like you're getting the hang of this," Clover shouted, nodding approvingly.

"I had a good teacher," Tara smiled.

It took the group about twenty minutes to cover the distance to the remote island, and when they got closer, they gaped at the tall mountains covered in thick, dense foliage. The flora this far out to sea was much more tropical, with tall palm trees and brightly colored fruit trees creating a patchwork quilt of colors. As they sailed along the sandy seashore, they breathed in the warm scent of the rainforest, looking for a place to land.

"Why don't we put down there?" Clover said, pointing to a pretty lagoon with a white beach.

"I don't know," Tara said, scanning the area for any sign of civilization. "We don't know if this island is inhabited. Maybe we should find a place higher up, at least until we know it's safe."

Tara peered toward a nearby peak, noticing a rocky outcropping where they could land.

"Maybe one with a *cave* where our two dragons can build a nest?"

She pulled back on Betty's ears and tilted her body in the direction of the escarpment, with Rex following close behind. When they reached the outcropping, the dragons fluttered down softly onto the ledge, and the three friends disembarked, peering out over the lush paradise.

"Yeah," Clover nodded, tracing her hand over the luminescent veins lining the rock. "This looks like a good spot for these two to begin building a new life. Maybe *us* too. I could get used to living in a place like this."

"It looks like there's plenty of food," Jessop said, appraising the abundant banana and citrus trees coating the side of the mountain. "Though I don't know how much wild *game* there might be to feed two full-grown dragons."

Tara noticed Rex and Betty nuzzling their faces together as they sat down next to one another.

"Why don't we leave these two lovebirds to set up shop while we scope the place out? They could probably use a little privacy now that they've established connubial relations."

"I'm developing a bit of an appetite of my *own*," Clover said, peering down at the turquoise lagoon. "I haven't had fresh seafood for quite a while, and that sandy cove at the base of the mountain looks like a great spot for a barbeque."

"Good idea," Tara smiled. "I'm eager to test those fishing skills you keep bragging about."

It took the trio the better part of two hours to make their way through the thick jungle down to the beach, and for the first thirty minutes or so they were content to play in the breaking waves and lie on the warm sand while they breathed in the salty air.

"So?" Tara said, turning to look at Clover through squinted eyes. "Are you going to catch us some dinner or what?"

"It's not going to be quite as easy as back in Tennessee," Clover said. "I lost my fishing rod along with everything else when I fell through the portal near your treefort. It's going to take a while to fashion a new one out of tree branches, some twine, and a pointy fishbone."

"The hell with *that*," Tara said, standing up and dusting herself off. "I've got a better idea. But it's going to take all *three* of us to catch enough to feed everybody."

After Tara explained her plan for corraling the fish, the three friends set about building a dam on one side of the lagoon using large rocks, then they began flailing the surface of the water, steering the fish toward the shallow water. Then Tara deftly speared a couple of large groupers and began filleted them on the beach while Jessop and Clover built a fire. As they sat down in a circle, pulling off the succulent flesh of the roasted fish with their fingers, Clover hummed in satisfaction.

"I'll be damned if this isn't the best fish I've ever had!" she gushed, smiling at Tara. "You never cease to amaze me with your survival skills."

Jessop suddenly jerked his head and widened his eyes, peering at a large band of scantily clad women approaching the trio with makeshift spears and bows.

"We might need some *more* of those pretty soon," he said.

Tara turned to gaze at the women then slowly stood up, motioning for the others to back away.

"Just be cool," she said. "We're no threat to these people.

I'm sure we can ease their fears once we explain what we're doing here."

"Right," Jessop said while his eyes darted over the women's taut, athletic figures. "Just don't mention the two *dragons* we've got squirreled away on the other side of the mountain."

3

———

"What are you doing here?" the statuesque leader of the group said.

"We were just having a snack," Tara said, trying to act calm. "Would you like to join us? There's plenty to go around–"

"No," the woman said, scanning the perimeter of the lagoon. "I mean, *how* did you get here? I don't see any boat."

"Um, we were shipwrecked," Tara said, scrambling to come up with a plausible explanation. "Our boat was capsized in a storm and we drifted here holding onto some logs."

"You don't *look* like you've been out at sea very long," the woman said, eyeing the trio suspiciously.

"Luckily, the tradewinds brought us here relatively quickly," Tara said, continuing her improbable charade.

"Well, you're going to have to *leave*," the woman said, thrusting a yellow-tipped spear into the sand beside them. "This is *our* island. And we don't take kindly to visitors. Especially *men*."

Tara took a moment to appraise the woman and her

bandmates. They were considerably taller than most regular women, with well-developed muscles and skimpy animal skin bikinis. And every one of them was drop-dead gorgeous, like they'd evolved into some kind of super-race of females on the isolated island.

At least there's some wildlife on the island to keep the dragons fed, she thought.

"How will we get off?" she said, not quite ready to reveal the truth about how they really got there. "The mainland is many miles away."

"The same way you *got* here," the woman said, raising an eyebrow. "The westerly winds will eventually take you ashore."

"May we at least spend the night here?" Tara said, trying to buy a little more time. "We're pretty exhausted after our ordeal, and we haven't eaten in days."

The woman turned to consult with rest of her clan and most of them nodded in assent.

"I suppose so," the woman said. "But you'll have to return with us to our village. I don't trust that you won't escape to the interior if we leave you alone. This is a big island, and there are many hiding places."

"Fair enough," Tara said, happy to deescalate the situation. She glanced over at Clover and Jessop and they both shrugged, unsure how else to proceed.

The leader led the threesome in a single line through a path in the woods with three other clanswomen taking up the rear to make sure they stayed in line. After ten minutes or so, they broke into a clearing with a collection of straw huts and women cooking around a fire while they wove baskets and other domestic goods. When they reached the center of the clearing, the leader motioned for them to sit around the fire where a few of the women handed them stone plates containing roasted game and fresh fruit.

"Thank you for your hospitality," Tara said. "Do you mind my asking why there only seems to be *women* in your tribe?"

"We've found that men only create trouble and treat women as slaves," the leader said. "All they seem interested in is power and domination. We've led a peaceful life here on the island of Sappho for many generations and have no need for them."

Tara turned her head, noticing a few young girls running playfully around the courtyard.

"How do you, um, *propagate*?"

"On the rare occasions that men come ashore to our island, we use them for the only thing they're good for then send them away," the woman said.

"What about the male babies? Do you send *them* away too?"

"Unfortunately, yes. In our experience, young boys just grow up to be violent men."

"So you send them out to sea all *alone*?"

"Like you said, the tradewinds will eventually take them to the shore. I'm sure somebody finds them and takes them in. But if not, the fewer men in this world, the better."

Wow, Tara thought to herself. *These Sapphic women don't fool around.* In a way, she admired what the clan had built on their isolated island. She'd had her own unpleasant experience dealing with domineering tribal leaders, and it was one of the reasons she'd set out on her own. But sending newborn babies out to sea in the hope they'd survive shark attacks and inclement weather seemed a little harsh.

"I assume you've fashioned some kind of makeshift

liferaft that we might use to make our return to the mainland?"

"We can build one large enough for the three of you if you wish," the woman nodded, motioning to two other clanswomen who excused themselves to begin collecting the necessary provisions.

"Since we'll be staying the night, I suppose we should introduce ourselves," Tara said. "My name's Tara and these are my friends Clover and Jessop."

"My name is Keke," the woman said, noticing Tara's pointed ears poking up through her short hair. "Are your friends elves like you?"

"No," Tara chuckled. "Though I sometimes think they *want* to be."

"That's good," the tribal leader said. "We will need Jessop's seed to be pure. Our fertile women haven't been inseminated for quite some time now."

Tara peered over at Jessop, who'd been suspiciously silent up to this point, and smiled.

"What do you think, Jessop?" she said. "Are you up for the challenge? There appears to be quite a few women of child-bearing age here."

"You're twisting my arm," Jessop smirked, rolling his eyes over the voluptuous figures of the women sitting around the fire. "But if it's in service of supporting the tribe, I'm willing to do my part."

"Good," Keke said, motioning to five young women in the circle who suddenly stood up. "These women will lead you to your quarters. We don't want you to spill any of your valuable seed. The more partners you have for each encounter the better."

As Jessop's eyes opened wide as saucers, one of the

women held out her hand, then practically yanked him off the ground, leading him toward one of the huts.

Tara smiled as she watched him being led away while he peered back at his friends like he'd died and gone to heaven.

"What do you women do to amuse yourselves during those long periods when there are no men on the island?" Tara asked Keke. "I mean, how do you satisfy your sexual needs?"

"It doesn't take a *man* to properly satisfy a woman," the tribal leader chuffed. "In fact, we've found that *women* are far more capable of pleasing another woman sexually. We've developed quite a robust set of techniques that men could only dream of."

"Oh?" Tara said, lifting an eyebrow as she peered over at Clover, who suddenly shifted uneasily in her cross-legged position on the ground.

"It looks like you and your friend have experienced your *own* share of woman-to-woman relations, judging by the way you're looking at one another," Keke said. "Would you two like to join me in my cabin tonight? Perhaps we can learn a few new techniques from each other. I've never been with an *elf* before."

Tara glanced at Clover to gauge her reaction, and she simply stared back at her friend with her mouth agape.

"That would be lovely, thank you," Tara smiled, hardly believing their luck stumbling upon this clan of sex-crazed women. "After our *last* experience, it will be a pleasure to mingle with someone closer to our own size."

After everybody finished eating, Keke led Tara and Clover back to her hut, where she quickly stripped, awaiting the other girls to do the same. She stood at least six feet tall, and with her broad shoulders, large globe-shaped breasts, and tight, muscular ass, she looked like some kind of super woman. After the two friends removed their outfits, Keke paused to appraise their figures, lingering for a few seconds longer than usual staring at their crotches.

"Why does the redhead have so little hair between her legs?" she said, pinching her eyebrows together as she stared at Clover. "Is she not yet of child-bearing age?"

"It's a weird custom they have in the land she comes from," Tara chuckled. "The women there shave their pubic hair to expose their vulvas. She's only had a little over a week or so to grow it back."

"I like it," Keke smiled. "She has a very pretty pussy. And I noticed that you have white hair on your pelvis. Are you older than you appear?"

"As a matter of fact, I am," Tara said. "We elves live considerably longer than the average human, and we also age more slowly. I'm over a hundred years of age, but still have the body of a young adolescent."

"Mmm," the tribal leader hummed. "I like indulging in a little juvenile pussy from time to time. Why don't you girls lie on my thatch mattress and show me how you play with one another while I figure out which one of you I'd like to fuck first."

"Okay," Tara said, peering at Clover as she cocked her head. "Maybe if we lie down in a scissor position with our bodies facing up, she can get the best view..."

"Works for me," Clover said, already beginning to feel her juices dripping down the inside of her thighs in anticipation of touching the voluptuous island woman.

The two friends lay down on the soft straw mattress then spread their legs apart, pulling their hips together. When their vulvas touched, they placed their arms at their sides and clasped hands, pulling their pussies tighter together.

"It looks like you've done this before," the tribal leader smiled, grabbing her crotch with one hand while she pulled one of her breasts upward with the other. "You two look like quite a snack rubbing your bodies together on my bed."

"*Snack?*" Tara said, peering up at the tall Amazon standing above the them.

"Don't worry," she laughed. "We're not cannibals. I'm not going to *eat* you. At least not in the way you're thinking."

She kneeled down over Tara's chest, straddling her knees beside her face, then she leaned forward, rubbing her dripping snatch over Tara's trembling breasts.

"I like your little elf tits," Keke grunted. "They fit perfectly inside my pussy. Hold them still while I spread my juices all over your hard nubs."

Tara grasped her breasts with her hands and pointed them higher in the air, then Keke pressed her hips down harder onto her chest, grinding her wet pussy all over her skin and pointed nipples.

"Yes, Tara," she panted. "Just like that. Let me fuck your pretty titties while I suck on your girlfriend's bosom."

As she leaned further forward, her ass tilted upward revealing her flexing rosebud, puckering in and out while she humped her hips against Tara's chest. The weight of her oversize frame almost suffocated the small elf, and she struggled to catch her breath whenever Keke raised her hips on each upstroke.

"Mmm," the tribal leader grunted, making loud

smacking sounds with her lips. "You've got pretty big teats for a girl your size, Clover. And I like the pink color of your flesh. It reminds me of the younger ones in our tribe."

By now, all three women were panting loudly from the combined friction on their dripping genitals, and Tara could feel Clover digging her nails into the side of her ass as she humped her hips more vigorously against Tara's wet cunt. Realizing she was getting close to climaxing with the pretty tribal leader sucking on her tits while she cunt-fucked her friend, Tara lifted her right hand and inserted three fingers into Keke's flexing pussy hole.

"*Fuck, yeah*," Keke panted, pulling her knees tighter against the side of Tara's head. "Fuck my pussy with your hand. Put it all the way inside me while I suck your friend's tits. I want you to feel me clamping down on your fist when I come."

Seeing how easily her small hand fit inside the Amazon's pussy, Tara curled her fingers into a ball and slid her knuckles past Keke's opening, beginning to ram her fist inside the woman's tightening pussy.

"Yeah, just like that," Keke panted. "You see, women can do everything a man can, and for much longer. Pound my cunt while I spray all over your face. I'm going to climax soon–"

Suddenly, the tribal leader emitted a loud howl as her powerful thighs clamped tightly around Tara's head while she squirted giant streams of musky juice all over her tits and face. While Tara blinked taking in the incredible view of the statuesque Amazon flapping her muscular ass atop her chest, she watched her butthole clamping with each powerful contraction the woman was feeling.

When she started to feel Clover gushing her juices over their connected pussies, she couldn't hold back any longer while all three women thrashed and wailed atop the squeaking mat. After what seemed like over two minutes of a prolonged and powerful simultaneous climax, Keke collapsed atop the two friends, panting in a wet, sticky heap, with her torso covering the entire length of their two bodies.

That's something I've never done before, Tara smiled to herself while trying to catch her breath with the weight of giant tribal leader still compressing her chest. *A three-way with two women while fisting one as she gushes all over my face. Maybe these Sapphic women have stumbled onto a good idea after all.*

4

———

The next morning, the three friends reassembled around the main fire pit with Keke and the rest of the Sapphic clan, enjoying a seafood omelette made with fresh quail eggs and fish harvested from the lagoon. Tara noticed that Jessop was crouching a little slower than usual, and she peered over at him as he gobbled down his breakfast.

"Are you trying to recharge your batteries after a long night of lovemaking, Jessop?" she kidded, nudging Clover in the side.

"Let's just say I've got a fair amount of *protein* to replenish," he smiled, looking at her sheepishly.

"We noticed you were walking with a bit of limp this morning," Clover smiled. "Are you sure you didn't pull a muscle or something trying to keep up with all these superwomen?"

"I'm surprised my tool is still functioning at *all* after the workout it got last night," he said, rubbing his sore crotch.

"How many women did you manage to service by the time you ran out of steam?"

"I lost track after the fourth or fifth group took their turn. Everything was done pretty much by hand so they could collect my semen and spread it around. Those tribal women sure have a powerful grip!"

"Poor baby," Tara teased. "It must have been just awful for you, getting jerked off by one beautiful woman after another while you watched them line up naked for you."

"It was pretty rough," Jessop chuckled, readjusting himself. "I'm not sure I'm going to be able to use this organ again for at least a week."

"I guess it's a good thing they'll be booting us off the island today then," Tara said, smiling at Keke. "Pretty soon you won't have to worry about so many beautiful women lining up for a piece of your body."

"Are you sure you don't want us to come back every couple of months to replenish your supplies?" Jessop said, peering over at the tribal leader.

"It takes nine months to produce a newborn," Keke smiled. "Then another twelve or thirteen years to raise them to childbearing age. So I don't think we'll be needing your services again for quite some time. But I thank you for your sacrifice."

"Don't mention it," Jessop grinned. "It was my pleasure."

Everybody chuckled, then Tara turned back to Keke with a more serious concern.

"Have you managed to build a raft to arrange our transfer to the shore?" she said. "I'm not sure we'll want to chance *swimming* our way back to the mainland in these shark-infested waters."

Keke motioned for two of the women to leave the circle and begin preparing the necessary provisions for the trip.

"The girls have built a liferaft that should carry you back there safely. They've even attached a small sail to expedite your journey." She threw some sand up in the air, watching it blow softly a few inches to her side. "The winds are blowing fairly strongly from the west today, so it shouldn't take you long to reach safe haven."

She paused to peer at the trio's tools lying beside them on the ground.

"Do you have anything else you wish to take back with you other than the clothes and weapons you brought with you?"

Tara hesitated for a moment looking at her two friends, knowing they were all thinking the same thing. They didn't want to leave their pet dragons behind without saying good-bye, but she knew it was probably best to leave them to their own devices so they could break free of their reliance on their human masters for food and support.

"Maybe just a bit of fruit and fresh water in case we get blown off course," Tara said. "Thank you again for your hospitality. I think it's fair to say that we all enjoyed our short stay here very much."

"I'm pretty sure I can say the same for the *rest* of the girls," Keke said, noticing some of the tribeswomen staring at Jessop's crotch while he finished his breakfast. "You've been a pleasant distraction for many of us during your stay here. I'm looking forward to sharing some of new techniques we tried last night with a few of the younger girls after you leave."

Tara smiled toward Keke as she panned around the circle at some of the younger women in the group. She had no idea when the tribe initiated them into their sexual practices, but she suspected Keke was already thinking about how their juvenile hands could be put to better use.

"I'm sure you *are*," she said, noticing the sun climbing higher in the sky. "If we'll be departing soon, I suppose we should leave while there's still good light. I'm not sure how well our liferaft will be able to navigate in the dark."

"I think you're right," Keke said, standing up with the rest of the clan as they escorted the trio to the lagoon, where a large liferaft rested on the side of the beach. "This should withstand the normal swells at this time of day."

Tara kneeled down onto the soft sand and pulled on the braided twine holding the hand-cut logs together. Just like the sturdy thatched mattress they'd cavorted on the night before, it appeared to be fashioned with the same precision and attention to detail.

"We've added a few paddles to help with your steering and assist with you getting out beyond the breakers," Keke said, motioning to the four-foot-tall waves cresting over the offshore reef.

"Thank you again for everything," Tara said, pushing the raft off the beach with her two friends. "Perhaps we'll see you another time the tradewinds blow us in your direction."

"You'd be advised to find a safer form of travel next time," Keke smiled. "The sea can get pretty angry at certain times of the year."

"Will do," Tara nodded, waving goodbye to the line of beautiful women standing on the beach as they drifted out of the lagoon.

<hr>

After the trio paddled past the waves cresting over the offshore reef, they raised the bamboo sail and turned the raft in the direction of the mainland.

"That was pretty wild," Jessop said, resting unsteadily on the bumpy surface of the raft. "Just when I thought you women couldn't get any more bossy and independent. That tribe of superwomen takes the concept of women's empowerment to a whole other level."

"Something tells me you weren't complaining too much while they were playing with your woody all night long," Clover smiled.

"I'm kind of getting used to letting you girls do all the work," he grinned, propping his elbow on the raft while peering up at the clouds rolling by in the sky. "But what about you guys? Judging by all the moaning and groaning coming from the adjacent cabin, it seems like you two were enjoying a little all-girl attention of your own."

"It was definitely pretty intense," Tara said, smiling at Clover. "At times it seemed like more of a *wrestling* match than a lovemaking session. My head is still ringing from Keke clamping her thighs around my face while she came all over my tits."

"Yeah," Clover said, rubbing her breasts softly. "And my nipples are still sore from her sucking on them like a newborn calf on its mother's teats."

"Everything they do here, it seems they do *big*," Jessop said, stretching his arms out over the generous swim platform.

"Not as big as the *last* group that held us hostage overnight," Clover chuckled, reflecting back on their previous experience in the giant castle.

"Hey," Tara said, suddenly pointing toward the leeward side of the island. "Speaking of *big*, what's that strange boat doing anchored on the other side of the island?"

Clover and Jessop squinted in the direction she was pointing, then Jessop looked back at his friends with a worried expression.

"That's a pirate ship," he said. "That's the *last* kind of

intrusion Keke and her tribe could possibly want on their island."

"What are they doing landing here?" Clover said, pinching her eyebrows together. "There's nothing on this island except a few fruit trees and some wild quail..."

"And *women*," Tara said. "Lots of beautiful, sex-starved women. Those sailors must be pretty horny after being out to sea for who-knows-how-long. And they're not exactly the placid, easygoing type like our friend Jessop, who's happy to let women take the lead. Those rapscallions are the very definition of the aggressive, chauvinistic men that Keke abhors."

"Maybe she'll welcome the new infusion of sperm to diversify their tribe..." Jessop said.

"I somehow doubt it," Tara said, shaking her head. "The women have got a pretty small tribe, and I suspect they just fulfilled their quota for the next couple of years. I'm afraid these intruders have more nefarious intentions."

"Want do you want us to do?" Jessop said, watching a large group of pirates offloading onto the shore.

"I think we should double back and see what they're up to," Tara said, motioning for him to drop the sail to keep them out of sight. "With that many heavily armed men, they could quickly overwhelm the tribeswomen and do who knows what to them."

"What about our dragons?" Clover said. "They could provide some useful aerial reconnaissance and help us out if things get a little dicey."

"There's no time to get them right now," Tara said. "It would take us hours to reach them on the other side of the island. Those men could plunder the entire village by the time we brought them into the fray. Let's set in around that bend then follow them under cover of the jungle to see what their plans are."

The three friends picked up their paddles and paddled vigorously in the direction of the bluff, then they camouflaged their raft with some palm fronds before heading back in the direction of the pirates' ship. When they reached the vessel, they discovered four empty skiffs pulled ashore and a large trampling of footprints in the sand.

"How many of them do you figure there are?" Clover said, peering at Jessop.

"Judging by the size of these dinghies, there could easily be sixty or seventy of them."

"That's more than the size of the women's tribe," Tara said, peering at the trampled path rising up from the beach. "And with their heavy weapons, they could easily overpower the women with the element of surprise. They've left a clear trail through the woods. Let's follow them to help our friends if need be."

"How exactly do you propose to do that?" Jessop said. "There's only three of us, and twenty times as many of them!"

"Yes, but we will *also* have the element of surprise approaching from their rear."

The threesome set through the forest with Tara in the lead, and when they reached the side of the island where the women had built their camp, they heard a loud commotion and the sound of women's screams. As they peered through the thick brush at the side of the clearing, they noticed the pirates binding the women's hands behind their backs, forcing them down onto their knees in the sand.

"What do you *want* with us?" Keke screamed, sneering at the pirate ringleader.

"We've found something very valuable on your island

that few people know about," he said, holding up a large rock glistening with bright yellow veins. "This place carries a motherlode of gold. We plan to stay as long as it takes to mine every last ingot."

"What is it with you men and this orange mineral?" she said, flailing against her binds. "It's too soft to make any useful weapons and too heavy to take anywhere."

"Yes," the pirate said, lifting Keke's yellow-tipped spear out of the sand. "But as you've already noticed, it's quite pretty and shines like nothing else. Where *I* come from, people value this ore very highly and I can exchange it for more ships, weapons, and men."

He pulled Keke's head back with his fist, pointing the tip of his sword toward her mouth.

"But of course, it's not just the *gold* we're interested in. There's *another* precious commodity on this island that's even more beautiful. After we finish pillaging your island of its gold, we intend to take our share of your *other* soft attractions before we leave."

"You'll never get away with this!" Keke wailed, spitting on the ringleader's crotch.

"We'll have to see about that," he snorted, peering at his fellow pirates. "These women appear to be a little more feisty than the skinny waifs we're used to. What do you say, men–shall we give them a little taste of our pirate bounty?"

"Aye, captain!" the rest of his clan snorted, waving their swords over the heads of the terrified women.

Tara turned to look at her friends with wide eyes, feeling her heart pounding in her chest.

"What do you want to do?" Jessop said. "I'm all for trying to save these women, but we're badly outnumbered."

"We just need to catch them at a vulnerable moment," Tara said, pausing as she began to form a plan. "The women are more than capable of dispatching these villains once their binds are freed–"

"I think I'm catching your drift," Clover smiled. "When do you want to make our move?"

Tara watched as the pirates began to drag the women one at a time into the surrounding cabins.

"Let's give them just long enough to get their pants down around their ankles," she said. "Once we catch them unawares, I'm pretty sure the Sapphites will take care of the rest."

"I like your thinking, Tara," Clover said, peering at her friend with a huge grin.

"Like Keke said," Tara nodded. "Men are only good for two things–oppressing women and seeking power. Women are the only ones capable of leading a peaceful, harmonious life."

"Where does that leave *me*, exactly?" Jessop said, shrugging his shoulders.

"Thankfully, you're not like the rest of them," Tara said, peering at the long blade hanging from the side of his hips. "At least you can be *trained* to recognize women as equals. Come on, let's see if we can find some use for that *other* sword of yours."

5

─────

After the pirates retreated into the cabins with the women, Clover peered over at Tara anxiously.

"Shouldn't we make our move soon?" she said. "I hate to think what those men will be doing to the women if we leave them in there too long."

"Ok," Tara nodded. "But we're going to have to work *together* to make it look like there's more of us than there really is. We'll attack from both sides of the courtyard, moving as quickly as possible from one hut to the next. You start at the south end, Jessop, and I'll work my way in from the other side while Clover strikes simultaneously in the middle."

Tara peered at Clover's coiled whip resting on her belt.

"Are you ready to use that thing for what it was really intended?" she said, staring at Clover intently.

"I've had plenty of practice using it to catch wild game," she smiled. "It shouldn't be too hard to disable a stationary target."

"Ok," Tara said. "Wait for my signal, then move quickly to surprise as many of them as you can. Hopefully, the women will pick up their weapons while they're distracted and take care of the rest."

The three friends split up, slowly approaching the cabins at their designated juncture points, then Tara held her arm in the air and flicked it to signal it was time to strike. Suddenly, the trio rushed into the cabins, lashing out with their assigned weapons, stunning and crippling the shocked and distracted pirates. While Tara flung a series of arrows into their bare asses and Jessop carved up their backs like Zorro, Clover lashed the tip of her whip between their legs, making them welp and roll over in horror.

When the tribeswomen saw the men doubled over in pain, they quickly scooped up their knives and swords, lashing at their genitals as the frightened pirates scrambled out of the huts back in the direction of their ship. Within minutes, the entire courtyard had been cleared of the assailants, while the women reconvened near the fire pit.

"Do you think we got them all?" Tara said, peering at the still-shaking tribal leader.

"I've never seen so many frightened men running for their lives," she chuckled. "Thank you for coming back to help us. How did you know they were here?"

"We saw their ship setting anchor on the other side of the island and suspected they were up to no good," Tara said. "We couldn't just sail by knowing they weren't exactly here on a humanitarian mission."

"I'm not sure we would have prevailed without your help," Keke said, motioning for a group of women to follow the fleeing men to make sure they left the island. "You're welcome to stay as long as you wish as our guests. It's the *least* we can do to thank you for your assistance."

"Maybe just for another day or two to make sure they

don't return," Tara said, noticing her friends nodding happily.

"Good," Keke said. "We'll have a big feast to celebrate tonight, then spread some more of the loving around if you three are up for some more lovemaking tonight."

"Oh, I'm definitely up for it," Tara smiled. "How about you, Jessop? Are you ready for a little more Sapphic hospitality?"

"I'm suddenly feeling a new rush of energy," he said, adjusting his lengthening pecker as he stared at the half-naked group of women standing in front of him.

W hen Keke's scouting party returned to report that all the pirates had quickly departed the island in their sailboat, the women set about pulling themselves together and preparing for the big feast later that evening. After the sun set, they all crowded around a giant fire in the center of the courtyard, gorging on wild boar and roasted quail while the tribeswomen put on a sexy dance in their skimpy costumes for their new friends.

"At least it looks like there's enough meat on this island to keep our *dragons* happy," Tara said, nodding toward the giant hog turning on the fire spit.

"It looks like there's enough meat on this island to keep *all* of us happy," Jessop said, watching the statuesque women shaking their muscular hips and large breasts to the beating rhythm of a pounding drum.

"*Jessop!*" Tara said, banging her fist against his shoulder. "Just when I thought you weren't like every other sexist man!"

"Come on," he said. "You can't tell me you two aren't also

fantasizing about all the things you want to do when you get these women alone later tonight."

"Perhaps," Tara said. "But I can assure you we won't be treating them like a piece of *meat*."

"Even if they want to wrestle you to the ground and try to suffocate you with their big muscles?"

"I'm sure we can find a few *other* ways to mix it up with the women tonight, am I right, Clover?" Tara said, turning toward her friend.

"Mmm," Clover hummed, distracted by the tribeswomen's undulating bodies just as much as Jessop. "I'm already fantasizing about licking every one of them."

"Who knows?" Tara said, smiling toward Jessop. "Maybe they'll let you poke them in some more *interesting* places tonight. It's not like they need to conserve your sperm any longer after everybody took a sample last night. You should be able to fuck them to your heart's content tonight."

"Hmm," Jessop smiled as he traced the dancing girls around the fire. "So many women, so little time."

When everybody finished eating, Keke stood up, holding a golden cup of homemade wine.

"I think we should make a toast to our new friends," she announced, raising her cup. "To Tara, Clover, and Jessop, who exhibited exceptional cunning and courage fighting off our adversaries. You'll always be welcome to visit our little clan whenever you're passing by."

"Thank you," Tara said, raising her cup and gulping down the wine with the rest of the group. "I'm not sure how soon we'll be visiting again, but it's good to know you've got our back if we stray off course."

"We'll have a lot more than just your *backs*," Keke smiled, turning to peer at Jessop. "But tonight, I think I'd like to take my measure of your *third* member. I admired his swordsmanship when he dispatched the pirates earlier today, and I'm eager to test out his *other* lance if he's still feeling capable."

"Oh, I'm feeling *capable*, alright," Jessop grinned, straightening his hardening cock under his sheepskin pants.

"Shall we retire to our huts for the evening, then?" Keke said. "If some of you girls want another piece of the boy, line up outside my hut and I'll be happy to share whatever he's got left when I'm finished with him."

Jessop's mouth gaped open as he peered around the circle watching all the tribeswomen smiling back at him expectantly.

"You might want to conserve your seed a little longer," Tara said, elbowing him in the ribs. "That is, if you want to sample *all* the meat before we have to leave."

"I'm *way* ahead of you," Jessop smiled, tilting his cock to one side to allow it to expand to its full length under his belt.

"Alright then," Keke said, leading him in the direction of her cabin. "Let the festivities begin."

When they disappeared into her hut, the rest of the clan divided into two large groups, leading the two girls into separate cabins.

"Try not to *break* anything in there," Tara said, winking at her friend as her group pulled her into one of the huts.

"Only my record for orgasms in a single night," Clover smiled.

After Keke closed the flap to her hut, she didn't wait for Jessop to strip, kneeling down in front of him and pulling off his pants while laying his sword on the floor. When she saw his large phallus spring up attentively against his belly, she flapped it from side to side with her hand, licking her lips.

"You've got a fair-sized tool there, Jessop," she grinned. "No *wonder* my bandmates were so eager to have another run at you tonight. I'm sure we can do better than caress you with only our hands this evening."

She engulfed Jessop's pole all the way down to his balls, tightening her lips and throat around his shaft as he groaned in ecstasy. While she bobbed her head up and down over his flexing abs, she curled her hand under his sac, squeezing his balls tightly. Jessop grunted and curled his fingers into Keke's long hair, pulling her face harder toward his pubis.

Suddenly she pulled her mouth off his twitching tool, glancing up at him.

"Whoa there, boy!" she said. "I don't want you getting any ideas about depositing your seed where it doesn't belong. I need to feel that big dick of yours somewhere *else* before you lose your energy."

"Wherever you desire," Jessop grinned, catching his breath. "My sword is at your disposal."

"Good boy," Keke smiled, pushing him down onto her mattress and straddling his hips with her knees.

Then she reached between her legs, grabbing the tip of his prick and rubbing it softly between her dripping folds.

"Mmm," she purred, peering down at him. "I can feel your syrup already oozing out of your hole. This is the way I like my men, underneath me where I can do whatever I want with them."

"Yes," Jessop panted. "Take me however you want. I want to plant my seed inside you while you rock your beautiful ass all over my balls."

"Oh?" Keke grinned, lowering herself a couple more

inches to take him partially inside her slit as she tightened her labia around his knob. "Do you like fucking girls bigger than you once in a while?"

"You have no idea," Jessop grinned.

"You're a little larger than most other men I've had," Keke said, pressing his dick further into her tunnel. "I like the way you fill me up inside."

Jessop raised his hips off the mattress, desperately trying to insert his cock all the way inside her, but Keke raised herself up a few inches, pressing him back down onto the mattress.

"Uh-uh," she said, shaking her head. "Remember who's in charge here. You're good when you're flashing your sword around other men, but when you're in *my* company, you need to know your place."

"You're a magnificent specimen," Jessop panted, ogling Keke's huge tits bouncing on her chest and her abdominal muscles flexing as she teased his cock. "I'm happy with my place, lying underneath the most beautiful woman I've ever seen."

"You really *are* different from other men, aren't you?" she said, angling forward to rest her hands on Jessop's hard pecs while she lowered her pussy further down his shaft. Once she rested her vulva all the way over his balls, she bent down, thrusting her tongue deep into his mouth.

"*Fuck* me with that weapon," she grunted. "Make me come all over your balls while I feel you shooting your seed inside me. You're going to produce some worthy offspring with that impressive set of features."

"Unghh," Jessop groaned, feeling his semen beginning to well up in his balls.

He could barely believe that he'd been able to get hard again so quickly after coming so many times the previous night, but the feeling of the gorgeous tribal leader rolling her voluptuous figure all over his naked body had taken him to new heights of pleasure. He was almost ready to come, but he wanted to hold back until Keke got off before he lost his erection.

"That's it, baby," Keke panted, flapping her big tits against his face while she hammered her pussy over his flexing organ. "Hold off just a moment longer–I'm almost there."

"Mhhh," Jessop hummed, trying to hold back the flood-gates while Keke gripped his dick even harder.

"Fuck, yes," Keke grunted. "I can feel your dick touching the end of my tunnel. Spray your nectar deep inside me. I'm going to come all over your beautiful, hard cock."

Jessop grabbed the sides of Keke's muscular ass with his two hands and thrust his dick as deep as he could into her dripping tunnel, tensing up his whole body.

"Ngah!" he growled, spurting his spunk deep inside Keke's pussy as he dug his nails into her side.

"Oh God," Keke hissed. "I can feel you spraying your seed inside me!"

She placed her hands on opposite sides of his face, practically sucking his tongue out of his mouth while she gushed her juices all over his shaking balls.

"Nnngh!" she groaned, compressing Jessop's face so tightly with her hands that he thought his head was going to explode.

It took over a minute for Keke to stop shaking overtop Jessop while she contracted her pussy over his pole, and when she finally finished coming, she sat up, smiling at him.

"You're pretty good at pleasing a woman," she said, turning her head to notice the lengthening line of tribeswomen waiting outside her door to have another turn at the handsome young swashbuckler. "Do you think you've got any *more* of that stuff to share with the rest of the girls?"

"I don't know about my *semen*," he said, feeling his tool still pulsing inside her pussy. "But I'm pretty sure I can at least stay *hard* long enough to satisfy a few more of them."

6

____

The following morning, everyone reassembled around the fire pit while they ate breakfast, smiling silently at one another around the circle. Nobody needed to say anything, remembering how they'd all shared partners during the all-night orgyfest. While the women seemed unusually content, Jessop groaned softly while he adjusted his position uncomfortably in the soft sand.

"How are you holding up there, sport," Tara said, noticing him massaging his aching groin.

"I don't expect any part of me will be _holding up_ again for quite some time," he grunted. "I think I've had enough sex to last me a lifetime."

"You say that _now_," Clover said, peering at the group of women gazing back at him affectionately from around the circle. "But something tells me these beautiful girls might coax a bit more life out of you if they twisted your arm."

"They twisted a lot more than just my _arm_ last night," Jessop chuckled, taking another bite of seafood from his plate. "What about you guys? It looks like you had your fair share of female attention *yourselves* last night."

"Indeed we did," Tara smiled, glancing at some of the girls gazing back at her knowingly. "I think all *three* of us might have had a turn with every one of these pretty women at least once by now."

"Are you growing *tired* of our female companionship?" Keke said, smiling toward Tara and Clover. "Perhaps you're looking forward to mixing it up with some more *men* once you get back to the mainland?"

"Quite the contrary," Tara smiled. "I don't think I've learned so many ways to stimulate a woman and be stimulated in return as I have these past couple of days. Are you in a hurry to get rid of us? Because I'm pretty sure there's still a few tricks we can learn before we go our way."

Keke turned her head, noticing one of her scouts running up from the beach with a worried look on her face.

"What is it, Maia?" she said when the girl stopped, panting heavily in front of the tribal leader.

"More ships!" she said, pointing out past the lagoon. "They look like the boat that was here yesterday!"

Everybody got up and ran toward the beach, then stopped at the edge of the shore, staring at the flotilla approaching from the west.

"There's *three* of them this time," Keke said, furrowing her brow. "Can you tell if they're pirate ships again?"

"They're carrying the same black and white flag," Jessop nodded as he squinted at the approaching vessels.

"How long do we have until they get here?" Keke asked.

"Thirty minutes, give or take," Jessop said.

"There'll be too many of them to defend yourselves," Tara said. "I think you and your band should retreat into the woods to take shelter."

"And *then* what?" Keke said. "Just *stand by* while we watch them pillage our island?"

"It's better than being raped and used as slaves," Tara said.

"Screw that," Keke said. "We Sapphites have never stood by while men tried to invade our home. We will fight them until our last tribe member if necessary."

"With wooden spears?"

"They took us by surprise last time," Keke said. "This time we'll be better prepared."

Tara peered at her friends uneasily. She knew the tribal women would be no match for this many pirates, even with their help.

"I have an idea," she said. "If you can hold them off for a little while, we might be able to bring in some extra reinforcements."

"What *kind* of reinforcements?" Keke said. "I thought you came here alone from a shipwreck?"

"Just *trust* us," Tara said, placing her hand on Keke's shoulder, peering into her eyes. "We haven't let you down before, and we're not about to now. We'll be back as soon as we can."

As the three friends dashed into the woods, Clover peered at Tara anxiously, knowing what she was thinking.

"Do you think we'll have enough time to reach them before the pirates overrun the village?"

"We'll have to," Tara said, peering up at the mountain where they'd left their dragons. "However long it takes us to get there, the return trip will be much faster. Let's just hope Rex and Betty are still there."

An hour or so later, the three friends hacked their way toward the dragons' escarpment, calling out their names to let them know it was friendly faces approaching. Suddenly, the two dragons peered out over the ledge, flapping their wings excitedly while they squawked like little hatchlings. As the trio climbed up over the embankment, the dragons rushed up to greet them, wrapping their wings around them while they wagged their tails.

"Rex!" Clover said, patting her dragon's neck while kissing the side of his face. "I've missed you so much! Have you and Betty been busy setting up home?"

"We haven't got time for happy reunions," Tara said, stroking Betty's belly where her scars were healing nicely. "We've got to get back to the village as quickly as possible to fend off the pirates. You fly Rex and I'll take Betty. Let's just hope they remember how to *maneuver* with us on their back."

The two girls hopped up on the dragons' backs, with Jessop positioned behind Clover. As they pulled back on the dragons' ears to direct them to take flight, the animals hesitated, unsure where their friends were taking them.

"Come on, Rex!" Clover said, digging her heels into his side. "Don't get cold feet now. We need you to save our friends!"

The two dragons stamped their feet in protest for a few moments, then they flapped their wings and rose up off the escarpment while Tara and Clover pushed their bodies forward, sending them diving down in the direction of the shoreline. As the girls steered the dragons toward the village, the trio could see the pirates streaming off the ships onto the beach while the band of women flung their spears in their direction. But it hardly seemed to slow their advance as the women backed up in a tightening circle toward the village square.

"We're barely going to make it in time!" Tara yelled over toward Clover, flying Rex at her side. "Let's split up and attack from opposite sides. But be careful not to harm the women when the dragons unleash their fire. We might only have one chance at this, so we better make it count."

Clover nodded as she peered at Tara, then she banked Rex a few degrees to the north while Tara tilted her dragon south. As they began to circle back in the direction of the courtyard, they saw the band of pirates closing in on the defenseless women crouching together around the fire pit.

"That's it, Keke," Tara smiled, banking Betty toward the open courtyard as she sailed toward the village. "Draw them all together where I can get a good shot at them."

She looked up and noticed Clover and Jessop swooping in from the other end of the courtyard, then she kicked her heels hard into Betty's sides, causing her to screech as she laid down a giant torch of flame onto the sand as the frightened pirates peered up, hardly believing their eyes. As they scattered in every direction trying to escape the approaching firewall, the two dragons swooped down over them, searing them like fried bacon while they ran around trying to fan their flaming clothing.

Suddenly, Keke and her band of tribeswomen rushed forward with logs and stones they picked up from around the fire, bashing the disoriented pirates over the head. As Tara and Clover angled their dragons to make a return pass, the pirates began running back toward their ships en masse, trying to escape the overhead menace.

"Wrong move," Tara hissed, banking Betty in the direction of the ships, passing over one of them as her dragon sent a giant fireball over it, slicing it in half.

Noticing that Tara was trying to cut off their escape, Clover swooped in from the other direction, directing Rex to blow his flame at one of the other ships, sending it aflame in a giant fireball. As they watched the rest of the pirates paddling frantically out to the last ship, the two girls glided up beside one another, turning to face each other.

"Should we cut the rest of them down and sink the last ship?" Clover said.

Tara paused for a moment as she peered down at the screaming pirates clamoring aboard the vessel and hastily trying to raise their sails.

"We're not barbarians like these pirates," she said. "I think we should let these ones go as a warning to their friends that we're prepared to defend this island at any cost."

Clover looked over her shoulder at Jessop, who nodded in agreement.

"I'm pretty sure after getting a taste of our dragons' fire that they want to come back here anytime soon," he said. "Let's go see if the girls are alright."

After making one more flyby to make sure the last of the pirates had paddled out toward the remaining boat, they steered their dragons back in the direction of the courtyard, landing softly beside the astonished tribeswomen peering up at the giant dragons with wide eyes.

"Just in time to save the day once again," Keke said, glancing at the dragons as they kneeled down to let the trio dismount. "Where in heaven's name did you find these creatures?"

"I have to be honest with you," Tara said, peering at Keke sheepishly. "We didn't actually come to your island from a shipwreck. We flew here with these two dragons. I didn't want to tell you right away because I wasn't sure how you'd react to another intrusion on your island."

"That was probably a good idea," Keke said, staring at the two dragons warily. "If we hadn't seen how you befriended them, we probably would have tried to kill them. How did you manage to tame them and train them to fly that way?"

"They're not so dangerous if you just show them a little love and maybe feed them once in a while," Tara said. "Come closer and I'll show you what I mean."

Tara held Keke's hand then pulled her gently toward her dragon, rubbing the side of Betty's neck softly.

"Here, touch her skin to show her you're not afraid of her."

Keke stepped forward slowly as Betty growled suspiciously, stroking the scaly skin over her front shoulder, trying to stay as far away from her giant teeth as possible.

"See," Tara smiled. "Dragons aren't so terrible once you get to know them. They're just like any other creature. If you show them some kindness, they'll happily return it in kind."

"You three are just *full* of surprises, aren't you?" the tribal leader said, motioning for the rest of her clan to approach as the two dragons sat down on their haunches, recognizing the band of women meant them no harm.

After the women cleaned up the square and buried the bodies of the dead pirates, they gathered around the fire pit once again to have a mid-day meal and discuss next steps.

"Do you think those men will come back again?" Keke said.

"I can't imagine they'd ever *want* to after seeing what these dragons can do," Tara said.

"Will you be taking them with you when you leave?"

"Actually," Tara said, glancing at her friends sitting next to her. "I think they've found a safe, quite home right here on your island. That is, if you and your clanswomen are willing to have them stay. We've found a secluded spot for them high on the mountain to build their nest."

"Oh?" Keke said, widening her eyes. "Are you expecting baby dragons?"

"These two have become pretty amorous of late," Tara smiled, noticing Rex and Betty curled up close to a group of tribeswomen on the other side of the circle. "I wouldn't be surprised if some little critters popped out sometime in the near future."

Keke smiled watching the dragons nibbling on chunks of omelette a few of the girls were holding out for them.

"They could prove to be quite useful if those pirates get any more ideas," she said. "And the girls seem to be taking quite a liking to them."

"Just be careful about feeding them too often," Tara chuckled. "They can get quite attached to you if you don't let them fend for themselves. Then you'll never have any peace and quiet in your little village."

"Can you show me how to *fly* them?" Keke said. "That way, at least I'll know what to do if there's another invasion of our island."

"Of course," Tara said. "It's easier than you might imagine. Would you like to go for a little test drive?"

"Sure," Keke said, noticing Rex eating out of the hand of one of the women. "Can we bring another one of my girls with us? Having *two* capable pilots will be twice as effective as one."

"By all means," Tara said, motioning for Clover to bring Maia along with her on Rex.

<hr>

After the four women returned to the courtyard from their test flight, Keke hopped off Betty with Tara and smiled.

"I had no idea riding a dragon could be this much fun," she smiled. "Thank you for teaching us how to pilot them."

"It's pretty much like riding a horse," Tara nodded. "You just turn their face in the direction you want to go and angle your body to tilt them up and down, and off you go."

"I can see that now," Keke said, grinning as she watched Maia stroking the side of Rex's neck.

"So what happens now?" Jessop said, joining his friends beside the two dragons.

"I think it's time we took our leave," Tara said, rubbing her hand over Betty's fully healed scars. "This is no place for a man, no matter *how* much we may have enjoyed our short stay. Let's give these beautiful women back their privacy and allow them to resume their quiet life of solitude. Besides," she said, glancing down at Jessop's crotch. "If we stay here much longer, I'm afraid your pecker might fall off."

"We've enjoyed your visit very much," Keke chuckled. "And that goes for *all* of you. You're welcome to visit us again any time you're passing nearby. Shall we prepare your raft with new provisions for your trip to the mainland?"

Tara paused as she peered at her friends, then back toward the dragons.

"Would you mind if we took a ride on one of the *dragons* to get back? It will be safer and swifter, and we can say a proper goodbye before we part company."

"Our course," Keke said. "Don't you want to take *both* of them?"

"I think it's best we leave one of them here," Tara said. "Otherwise, they might want to keep following us. If we leave Rex with you, I'm pretty sure Betty will want to come back to raise their hatchlings together."

"That's a smart plan, like always," Keke smiled. "We're going to miss you, but the dragons will provide a welcome diversion from our usual activities."

Keke stepped forward and gave each of the friends a warm hug, then all of the tribeswomen surrounded the trio, giving them an impromptu tribal dance. When they finished, one side of the circle opened toward the lagoon, signaling their departure. The three friends stepped toward Rex, hugging and stroking his face as they said their final goodbye to their faithful sidekick.

"Goodbye, buddy," Jessop said, grabbing the sides of his cheek and pulling his face playfully from side to side. "You've been the best pet I've ever had, even if you let Clover do the driving all the time."

Then Tara stepped forward, caressing the sides of his jaw.

"Thanks for getting us out of that jam at the king's castle," she said, stroking him softly. "But I'm glad we were able to find a suitable mate. Take care of Betty while we're away, and hopefully we'll see you again before too long."

Then Clover stepped forward, peering into Rex's eyes as a tear streamed down her face.

"Oh, my dear, beautiful Rex," she said, curling her arms around his chin as she lay her face on his nose. "I'm going to miss you so much. But I know you'll be happy with your new girlfriend, and these lovely ladies will take care of you if anyone tries to do you any harm. Maybe the next time we come back, you'll have some grandchildren for me to play with. Goodbye, sweet boy."

As the three friends piled on Betty's back with Tara in the lead, Rex suddenly sat up, looking forward to going for another ride with his friends. But Maia stepped forward and held on to his ear, pushing him gently back onto the ground.

"You stay here with your new friends, Rex," Tara said. "We'll send Betty back to stay with you in a little while. "We're just going to go for a little ride, then you can live happily ever after in this amazing new place. See you soon."

As Tara pulled back on Betty's ears and motioned for her to take flight, Rex watched his friends fade away into the distance as they headed toward the mainland on the eastern shore. When they finally got there, they landed on a secluded beach, where the three friends dismounted and said their goodbyes to their other pet dragon.

"Okay, girl," Tara said, pointing back in the direction of the small dot on the horizon. "You go back to be with Rex. He'll take care of you and protect you from those nasty drag-onslayers. You guys better get busy and produce some more little dragons. Who knows how many more men will want to come back after they hear about all the gold on that island."

Betty looked at them inquisitively, then she peered out to sea, focusing on the little island in the distance. Tara slapped her behind softly, and she flapped her wings while the three friends pointed for her to head back to the island. As she took flight and headed back out to sea, the trio waved goodbye, not knowing when they'd see her again.

"So where do we go now?" Clover said, watching Betty fade into the distance. "It feels kind of strange not having our usual mode of air travel to get around."

"I guess we'll just have to *schlepp* it like everybody else," Tara smiled. "Unless you've got another one of those jet airplanes you can bring with you through the portal next time."

R*eady for more erotic chills and thrills? Order the next exciting volume in Clover's Fantasy Adventures:*

Some witches are bad, some witches are good, and some are devilishly good...

ALSO BY VICTORIA RUSH

Wet your whistle a hundred different ways with Jade's Erotic Adventures. Browse the full collection of Victoria Rush steamy stories here:

Click to scan your favorites...

FOLLOW VICTORIA RUSH:

Want to keep informed of my latest erotic book releases? Sign up for my newsletter and receive a FREE bonus book:

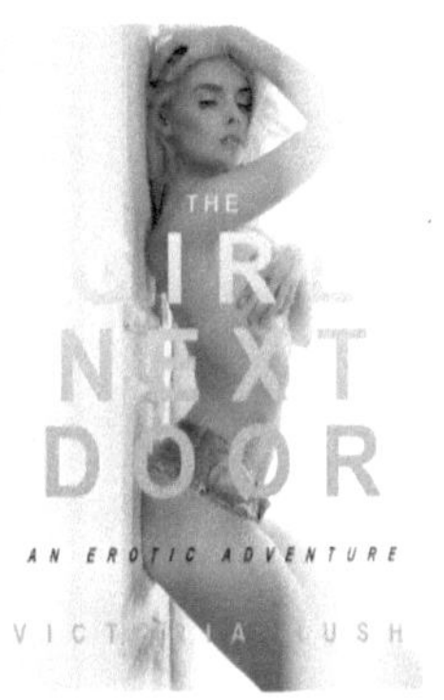

Spying on the neighbors just got a lot more interesting...